The Fruit Surprise!

How to Grow Fruit

Dr. Jasjit Delow

EWARIS
Mango

Radha likes
eating fruit.

Growing
Fruit

Today, she is reading a
book about how to
grow fruit.

Fruit comes from plants
Plants are living things.
All plants need sunlight, oxygen, and water to grow.
Plants make their own food to grow.

- Fruit comes from plants.
- Plants are living things.
- Plants grow from seeds.
- Plants need sunlight, oxygen, and water to grow.
- Plants make their own food to grow.

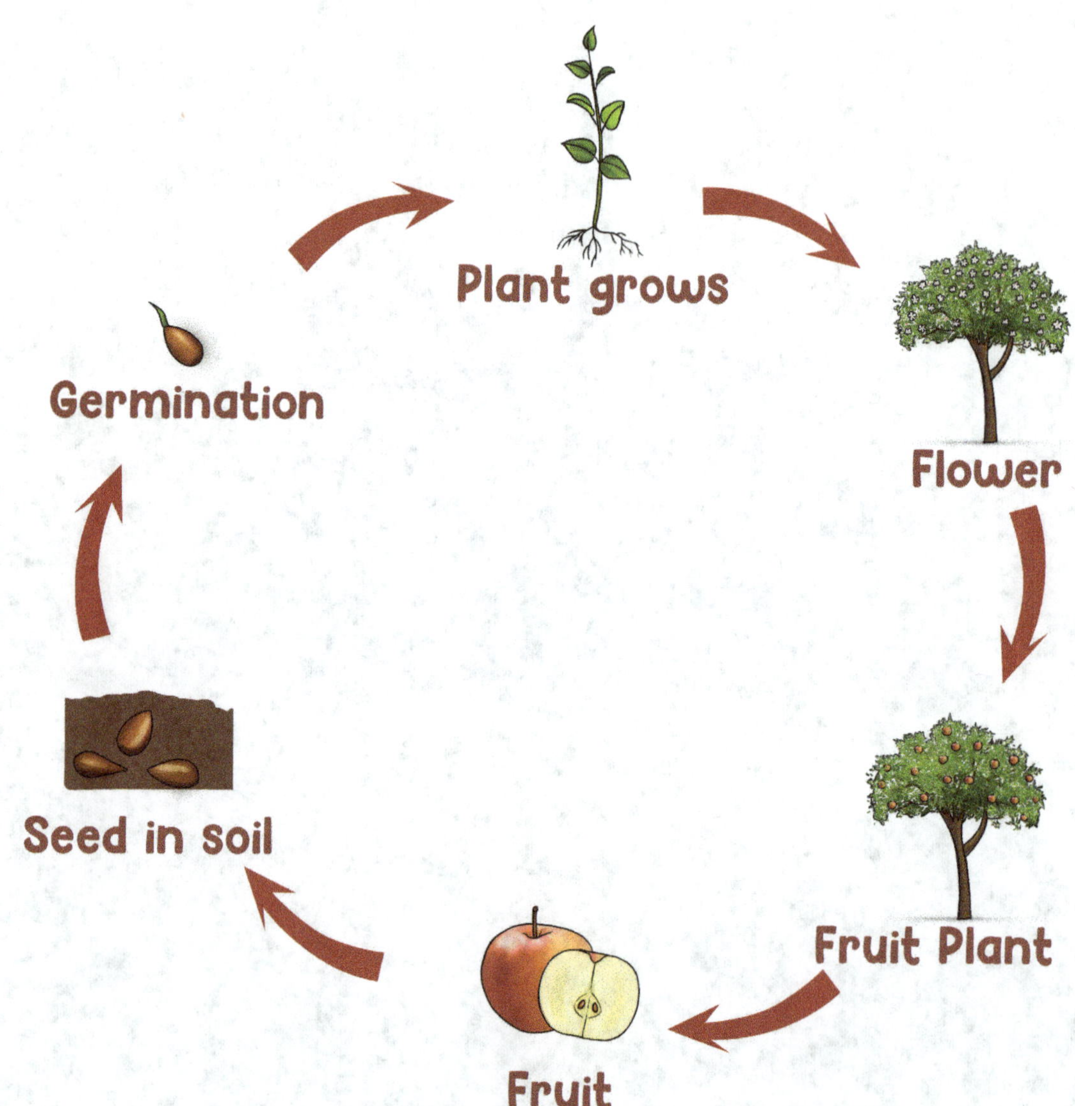

Plant grows
Flower
Fruit Plant
Fruit
Seed in soil
Germination

Radha reads the line,
"plants grow from
seeds."

Suddenly, Radha remembers eating watermelon, and she ate some of the seeds!

I drink water
I go out in the sun
I eat food
Oh No!

That night, Radha is still
thinking about eating
the watermelon seeds.

"Does that mean
watermelons will grow in
my tummy???" she cried.

Later that night…
Radha dreams that a
watermelon is growing
inside her belly, getting
bigger and bigger in her
stomach.

FLOUR

The next morning, Radha's
Dad calls to her.
"Radha, breakfast is
ready!"

A half watermelon is on the
kitchen counter.
The table is set with a plate
of watermelon with seeds.

Plant seed
Seedling
Plant with flowers
Sprout
Fruit on the plant
melon
Wat

Radha: "Dad, how do you grow watermelons?"
Dad: "Well, Radha, it's like a story – first, you plant a seed, it germinates into a sprout, becomes a seedling, grows with flowers, and eventually, you get watermelons!"

In the story, Radha is worried that, after eating some watermelon seeds, she might grow a watermelon in her tummy. Radha understands now that seeds need many things to grow. They need to grow in soil, and, they need oxygen and water. As they grow, they need sunlight to make food. So, she couldn't really grow a watermelon in her tummy after all. Thank goodness!

"Which is your favourite fruit?"
"Do you know how to grow it?

GLOSSARY

Fruit: It is a product of a plant that can be eaten as food. It mostly contains a seed.

Germination: Plant develops from seed. The process is called germination.

Grow: Something that can become larger or bigger in size. Fruit grows in soil when they receive sunlight, water, and oxygen.

Living things: The things that can grow, breathe, move. **Example:** Human, plants, animals, insects.

Oxygen: A gas that is important for life.

Plant: A plant is like nature's magic that grows from tiny seeds into beautiful living things that give us air, food, and joy!

Seed: A part of a plant from which new plants can grow

Soil: The part of the land where plants grow. Plants need nutrition from the soil to grow.

Sunlight: The light that comes from the sun. Most plants need to get their energy from sunlight.

About The Author

Jasjit Delow is a teacher in Canada with roots from India (Punjab). Jasjit is somewhat shy to speak in front of the audience, so she tries to reveal her feelings in her writings . When she was little, she used to day dream a lot and make her imaginary stories. Radha character is close to Jasjit as she also likes to day dream and make her imaginary creations. Dreams helps us to travel to another world without any cost. So, never stop dreaming.

www.ingramcontent.com/pod-product-compliance
Lightning Source LLC
Chambersburg PA
CBHW080424010826

48976CB00020B/2691